KT-438-405

SOCCER SQUAD

★ STARTING ELEVEN

Bali Rai

Illustrated by Mike Phillips

RED FOX

SHETLAND LIBRARY

SOCCER SQUAD: STARTING ELEVEN
A RED FOX BOOK 978 1 862 30654 7

Published in Great Britain by Red Fox,
an imprint of Random House Children's Books
A Random House Group Company

This edition published 2008

1 3 5 7 9 10 8 6 4 2

Copyright © Bali Rai, 2008
Illustrations copyright © Mike Phillips, 2008

The right of Bali Rai to be identified as the author of this work has been asserted
in accordance with the Copyright, Designs and Patents Act 1988.

All rights reserved. No part of this publication may be reproduced, stored in a retrieval
system, or transmitted in any form or by any means, electronic, mechanical,
photocopying, recording or otherwise, without the prior permission of the publishers.

Set in 14/22pt Meta Normal

Red Fox Books are published by Random House Children's Books,
61–63 Uxbridge Road, London W5 5SA

www.**kids**at**randomhouse**.co.uk
www.**rbooks**.co.uk

Addresses for companies within The Random House Group Limited can be found at:
www.randomhouse.co.uk/offices.htm

THE RANDOM HOUSE GROUP Limited Reg. No. 954009

A CIP catalogue record for this book is available from the British Library.

Printed in the UK by CPI Bookmarque, Croydon, CR0 4TD

'Get organized, lads!' Mr James shouted from the touchline. 'Four-four-two, like before!'

Steven got the ball in midfield and passed it onto Jason, who dribbled it past two of their players. Then he pushed it forward to Abs. Adam was right behind Abs but didn't make a tackle. Abs faked to turn to his left but instead swivelled and went right, leaving Adam standing.

Abs looked up and let go a powerful shot which sailed just over the bar . . .

SHETLAND LIBRARY

91132143

Don't miss any of the books in this fabulous
football series:

Available now:

SOCCER SQUAD: STARTING ELEVEN
SOCCER SQUAD: MISSING!

Coming soon from Red Fox:

STARS!
GLORY!

Chapter 1

Monday

'Make sure you eat all of your lunch,' Mum shouted as I left the house.

'OK!' I replied as Chris grinned at me.

'That's exactly what my mum said to me,' he said.

My name's Dal and Chris is my best mate. We've known each other since infants – he's like my brother, and we always do every-thing together.

We walked down my road, Persimmon Drive, and round onto Ethel Street, towards our school, Rushton Juniors. Rushie for short. It was horrible being back at school. The summer holidays went by so quickly! It was like they had never happened. But at least we had football to look forward to. And we *loved* football. I yawned as we got to the school gates.

'You could get an elephant in that hole,' said Chris. 'A whole *herd* of elephants.'

Chris is always making really *bad* jokes. He's well known for it.

'A *big* elephant – like my sister?' I asked jokingly.

'No, bigger. About the same size as *my* sister!' replied Chris.

Our sisters, Jas and Veronica, were best friends too. They were both fourteen. Four years older than us. They were *weird* – always talking about boys and make-up. Or sending each other texts and instant messages. At the same time!

'Good job they ain't here,' he said. 'Veronica would go crazy if she heard me call her an elephant.'

'I know. Do you remember when you found her mobile phone and sent those texts to her boyfriend? She was really angry,' I replied.

'Yeah – she made me do all the house-hold chores for a month so she wouldn't tell Dad.'

Chris grinned. Then I asked about football – or rather *The Football*. We went to a local youth club and they had an under-elevens football team called the Rushton Reds. We both *really* wanted to play for them this season and the trials were this week.

'The notice said tomorrow – at the youth club,' Chris told me.

'I've got new boots,' I said proudly. 'The same ones that Steven Gerrard wears.'

'I got new boots too,' replied Chris. 'My

dad got them from Rushton Sports in town.'

'Do you think we'll get into the team?' I asked.

Chris nodded. 'We should do. We're the best in our school.'

'I hope we do,' I said.

I was feeling a bit nervous about the trials. I mean, I knew we were good players – we were great at football. But what if we weren't good *enough*? What if my mates made it and I didn't? I'd be gutted. I *had* to play for the Rushton Reds!

'We'll be OK,' said Chris. 'As long as we play our best, we'll be fine. And with new boots too. It'll be *easy* . . .'

I hoped so.

At school we met up with Abs and Jason. They were mad about football too and the four of us were going to the trials together. They were standing by the school gates. Abs smiled at us. His black hair was shaved to his head and there were lines cut into it which started at his temples and ran round to the back of his head. Tramlines, they're called.

'We battered them!' he was saying to Jason, talking about his favourite team, Manchester United.

'No you didn't – I saw it on *Match of the Day*. You were lucky. It was never a penalty.'

Jason was the tallest. His blond hair was in a new style too – gelled into stiff spikes. He's got freckles and a mouth that looks too big for his face. And his ears stick out. But he's brilliant at football even if some of the other boys call him 'Jughead'.

'It was a *definite* foul!' replied Abs, still going on about the game. 'It's not like when Chelsea play. The ref always helps them . . .'

Jason raised his eyebrows at the mention of *his* favourite team. He winked at me and

Chris before answering. 'Just 'cos your team isn't the only good one any more!' he said. 'You should learn to be more humble, Abs.'

'Bet you don't even know what that means!'

Jason just shrugged. 'I don't. I just heard the manager say it on *Match of the Day*,' he admitted.

'Cabbage-faced glory hunter,' said Abs.

The rest of us looked at each other before bursting into laughter.

'What?' asked Abs, looking confused.

'Cabbage-faced?' said Chris. 'Where'd you get that . . . ?'

At lunch time I didn't wait for the other lads. I was starving and they wouldn't hurry up. Instead they were having the same conversation as before, about the Premier League and what had happened over the weekend. Only this time Chris was talking about *our* favourite team, Liverpool FC. I was the first to get to the dinner hall and I went straight for the sausages and chips – my favourite. The dinner lady knew me and she was really nice.

'Do you want an extra sausage and some more chips, love?' she asked me.

'Yes please, Miss Jones!' I said.

She gave me three fat sausages and a pile of chips. My plate looked like it had a small mountain of food on it. The smell was amazing and I'd put loads of tomato ketchup on it too! My stomach was rumbling even before I'd sat down. By the time the other lads had joined me, I was nearly halfway through my lunch.

'We wondered where you'd gone,' said Chris as they sat down with their lunches too.

'I was *hungry*,' I explained. 'And besides, you were talking about the same things as before.'

'Abs was saying Liverpool are rubbish,' Chris told me.

'They *are*!' said Abs through a mouthful of pizza. Bits of it flew out and landed all over the table.

'*Ehhh!*' said Jason. 'Can't you wait until after you've swallowed your food?' he asked. 'My mum would kill me if I did that.'

'She's not here though, is she?' replied Abs.

'That's not the point,' said Jason, going red and looking a bit angry.

'Oh, stop arguing,' I told them. 'Let's talk about something else . . .'

'Yeah, like how your team was lucky to beat Aston Villa four–nil on Sunday,' said Jason, his face becoming one big silly grin.

Despite not wanting to talk about the weekend I couldn't help myself. Jason was talking about Liverpool and they were my favourite thing ever. There wasn't a song or a

TV show that matched them. There was no way he was going to get away with it, even though we spent ages every day winding each other up.

'*Lucky?*' I asked. 'How can it be *lucky* when we scored four goals? *Four!*'

I held up four fingers to show Jason exactly what I meant.

'Lucky . . .' replied Jason, only this time he said it quietly.

'EAT YOUR LUNCHES IN SILENCE!' came a shout from behind us.

We didn't need to look to know who it was. It was Mr Williams, the deputy headmaster, and he was always shouting at everyone.

'I bet he even shouts at home,' said Chris in a whisper.

I nodded.

'*Get me my slippers! Where's my toast?*' Chris said in a slightly louder voice.

'I feel sorry for his wife,' said Jason.

'He's too ugly to have a wife,' added Abs.

We laughed as quietly as we could manage and then I went back to worrying about the football trials.

Chapter 2

Tuesday

We spent the whole of the next day talking about the football trials, which started straight after school.

'I hope I can play in my best position,' Abs said during morning break. 'I love being a striker!'

'What – from the bench? Because that's where you'll be watching us play from!' asked Chris, before opening a bag of cashew nuts. He was always eating nuts.

'Leave it,' said Abs. 'Your jokes are

rubbish.' He pulled a face.

'Like *your* jokes?' replied Chris. 'You tell some of the unfunniest jokes in the world.'

'I don't think "unfunniest" is a proper word,' Jason said.

'Yes it is – my sister uses it,' replied Chris, throwing a cashew nut at Jason.

Jason dodged and the nut flew past his head. 'Oi!' he shouted as Chris smirked.

'Bet it's not in the dictionary,' continued Abs, still going on about the word 'unfunniest'.

'You think the other players will be better than us?' I asked, changing the subject to something *I* wanted to talk about.

'*No!*' said Jason.

'How do you know?' I added, pleased that they seemed so sure.

'Because we're *too* good,' replied Abs.

'When we play at the park we're always the best ones there.'

'My dad showed me this Brazilian lad on YouTube,' said Chris. 'They call him "The Seal". He was running with the ball on his head.'

'*No way!*' the rest of us said together.

'It's true. I'll show you if you like. He was wicked,' replied Chris, before stuffing some more nuts into his mouth and crunching on them noisily.

'I don't think *he's* going to be there,' said Abs. 'Or Wayne Rooney.'

Jason groaned. 'Trust you to bring a United player into it,' he said.

'We were talking about the best,' Abs told him. 'So I mentioned *the* best.'

I told Abs and Jason to shut up.

'We aren't just going to walk into the team, are we?' I added.

'Prob'ly,' replied Chris.

'But we have to show the coach what we can do,' I insisted.

Abs shrugged. 'We will,' he said, acting confident.

'Yeah – and what if you don't make it?' I asked him, starting to sound like a skipping CD.

'P.M.A.,' he replied.

'Huh?' asked Jason.

'Positive Mental Attitude,' said Abs. 'My dad says that's what you need to succeed. We have to think like winners to be winners. That's how I know for certain that I'll play for Man U when I'm older.'

After school I walked home with Chris. When we got to my house, I saw my dad's car on the drive. He'd finished work early, just like he'd promised me.

'My dad's going to drive us to the trial,' I said to Chris.

'Nice one,' he replied. 'I'll just run home and get my kit.'

Chris lives around the corner and he was back in ten minutes, with a sports bag hanging from his shoulders. I was standing by the car with my dad when he arrived.

'Hello, Mr Singh,' Chris said to my dad.

'Hey, Chris,' replied my dad with a smile.

'Did you remember your new boots?' I asked my best mate.

'Yeah – my mum had my stuff ready for me. Are we picking up Abs and Jason too?'

'They're coming with Jason's mum,' my dad told him.

'I'm nervous,' I admitted.

My dad ruffled my hair. 'You'll be fine. Just do your best – you can't do any more than that.'

I nodded.

'Right – let's go!' Dad said. He looked more excited than me and Chris.

The drive to the youth club took ten minutes.

It was on the edge of Stoneygate Park and the football pitch was behind the clubhouse. We met up with Jason and Abs in the car park.

'Hi, Mrs Partridge,' I said to Jason's mum.

'Hello, Dal,' she replied.

'Are you staying to watch us?' I added.

'Of course I am,' she beamed. 'You'll be great – all of you.'

I nodded, looking around the car park for the competition. There were loads of cars and lots of other parents. And more importantly there were lots of other boys too.

I nudged Chris. 'Have you seen how many players there are?' I said.

'Yeah – I didn't think there'd be so many,' he told me.

I looked around again and my stomach started to do funny things. I was so nervous. But I held it in and took a few deep breaths. We could only do our best, I told myself, repeating what my dad had said.

There were fifty lads in total, according to Abs. He'd counted them. The coach, Mr Turner, came over. He was friendly looking but with a serious face. He split us into five groups for the warm-up. I was in the same group as Abs, but Chris and Jason were separate. We ran and did short sprints and then worked through a course of ladders and cones. Very quickly a few lads had to stop because they weren't fit enough and that made Abs laugh.

'We're going to breeze through this,' he whispered to me as we lined up to take another run through the ladders. 'Half of them are tired already and we haven't even started playing yet.'

Mr Turner blew his whistle and told us to stop. 'Stay in your groups and get two balls for each group,' he said, nodding towards a pile of footballs. 'I want to see what your juggling skills are like.'

Abs ran over to the balls and picked up two. He brought them back to our group and gave one to a lad called Steven.

'Split your group into two and form a circle each,' instructed Turner. 'I want to see the ball in the air. Two touches each. One to control the pass and one to lay it off. I do not want to see the ball touch the floor!'

We started doing what he'd asked. Straight away the ball hit the ground. We tried again and still we couldn't get it right. One boy, Dipesh, couldn't control it for toffee. Every time he got the ball it flew off him at weird angles.

'Come on!' shouted Turner. 'This is the easy bit!'

I decided to concentrate better. I took the ball and juggled it from foot to foot and then sent it looping into the air for Abs. Abs took it on his left thigh and then cushioned a

pass to Steven. Steven did exactly the same as Abs and the ball came back to me. I took it on my right foot and then passed to Dipesh. The ball came off his shin and shot off out of our circle.

'Dipesh!' shouted Steven and the fifth lad, Gurinder.

'Soz,' replied Dipesh, going red in the face.

Mr Turner blew his whistle five minutes later.

'That was horrible!' he told us. 'I asked you to do the simplest thing and half of you look like you've got lead shoes on. And you want me to put you in my team? I'd rather coach the girls!'

I looked at Abs and swallowed.

'This is going to be *really* hard,' I said.

Chapter 3

The training lasted for another twenty
minutes. Then it was time for a game.
Mr Turner split us up. He made two groups of
twenty because ten boys had already given
up. I smiled as he put Abs, Jason and Chris
into the same team as me. We also had
Steven, Gurinder and Dipesh on our side.
And a group of lads who we hadn't met yet.

'We should go and introduce ourselves,' I
suggested to Chris.

'Yeah – it'll be good for team spirit,'

replied Abs. 'Man U's manager is always saying how important team spirit is.'

'You sitting on the bench would be good,' joked Jason.

'Shut up, Captain Flowerpants,' said Abs.

I looked at Chris and we burst into laughter. Jason went red. Captain Flowerpants was Jason's *other* nickname after Jughead.

'That's an old joke,' he protested.

'Still funny though,' said Abs.

The joke about Captain Flowerpants had started the year before. We'd been doing PE at school and Jason forgot his shorts. Our teacher, Mr Warner, made Jason do PE in his pants. And his pants had little swirls on them that looked like flowers. We'd been ribbing him about it ever since.

I went over to the other boys and started to introduce myself and the others. As I was doing that another coach, Mr James, walked over to us. He'd been helping Mr Turner with the warm-up but hadn't spoken to us yet. He looked and sounded like someone you wouldn't mess with.

'OK, lads,' he said in a northern accent. 'Let's get you organized . . .'

He split us up into defence, midfield and attack, with Gurinder as the goalkeeper. That was Gurinder's position and he even had his own brand-new gloves with him.

'Wicked,' he replied, smiling.

Mr James randomly picked out eleven of us to start the game, but neither me nor Chris were in the team.

'*Sir!*' moaned Chris.

'Relax, son,' replied Mr James, 'you'll get your turn. It's rolling substitutes, which means that you'll be called off and sent on throughout the game. This is just the *first* trial. If you are asked to come back on Thursday, we'll sort out who plays where then. For today, just do your best . . .'

I looked at Chris, who smiled. He was obviously over his moan.

'Not everyone will make the squad,' added Mr James, 'but those of you who do should know that our first game is this Saturday morning . . .'

This time I smiled. A big, beaming smile. I couldn't believe the first game was so soon! It made me even more determined to play for the Reds. There was no way I wasn't going to play come Saturday. No way.

The game kicked off five minutes later and that was when we saw Adam for the first time. He was on the opposing side and he was *huge* – tall and wide. He looked fifteen years old, not ten, and I gulped.

'*Wow!*' said Chris in amazement when he saw Adam. 'He's a giant!'

'So?' said Abs, getting all cocky. 'He might be big, but can he play?'

'We're about to find out,' said Jason. 'All I know is, if he tries to tackle me I'm jumping out of the way!'

The lad called Adam walked slowly out onto the pitch and took up his position in defence. He'd be facing Jason and Abs, who'd both been given strikers' roles. He looked weird. Like his arms and legs were too big and he couldn't control them properly.

'*See?*' said Abs. 'He's like a big bear, Dal. We'll just pass the ball *around* him . . .'

Mr Turner started the game as me and Chris watched from the touchline.

'Keep stretching, lads,' Mr James warned us. 'You could be on any minute . . .'

I grinned as the action started. The other team passed the ball to each other, and Steven, who'd warmed up with us, tried *really* hard to get the ball back. But the rest of our team didn't do anything. They just let the other team play! Very quickly they were bearing down on our goal and it was the big lad, Adam, who had the ball. I looked across at the defence and groaned when I saw Dipesh and another lad called Danny playing there. Both of them had been rubbish during the warm-up and now they looked scared. I glanced over at Abs, who was running back to help the defence. His face was red and his arms were all over the place as he ran.

He was shouting: 'STOP HIM!'

Steven caught up with Adam and managed to get him to run wide of the goal but then Adam passed the ball to one of his team-mates. The lad who got the ball touched it past Dipesh and then put it through Danny's legs. Nutmegged! As Gurinder, our goalkeeper, came rushing off his line, the lad pushed it past him too, and into the back of an empty goal. Our entire team groaned and the other team cheered.

It was 1–0!

The ball went back to the centre circle, and Mr Turner, who was refereeing the game, blew on his whistle to restart the match.

'Get organized, lads!' Mr James shouted from the touchline. 'Four-four-two, like before!'

Steven got the ball in midfield and passed it on to Jason, who dribbled it past two of their players. Then he pushed it forward to Abs. Adam was right behind Abs but didn't make a tackle. Abs faked a turn to his left but instead swivelled and went right, leaving Adam standing.

Abs looked up and let go a powerful shot which sailed just over the bar. Another groan went up.

Abs shook his head and took up his position again. For the next ten minutes the ball went back and forth between our team and the opposition. But then Adam got hold of it again and he ran straight through our team. No one could stop him! He was left with only Dipesh to beat. Dipesh cried out as Adam ran at him, closed his eyes and swung out his right foot. But he kicked fresh air. Adam just went to his left and then shot into the bottom right corner, just past Gurinder's outstretched hand. It was 2–0!

Immediately Mr James told me and Chris to get ready.

'You're going into the defence,' he told us.

I smiled, because defence is my position, but Chris is a striker and he complained to Mr James. The coach shook his head and pulled Chris up.

'The first rule of the Rushton Reds,' he told Chris, 'is *teamwork*. I need you to play for the team – even if it is out of position.' Chris nodded slowly.

'Now get out there and sort things out at

the back. Get tight on their strikers and stop them getting any space. Understand?'

'*Yessir!*' said Chris.

Mr James called Dipesh and Danny off, and me and Chris entered the game.

'Come on!' I shouted to my team-mates. 'Let's start playing!'

Chapter 4

I was really confident when I ran onto the pitch with Chris. But within five minutes things got even worse! Their strikers, Dave and Harry, played the ball to each other a few times and even though I managed to tackle Harry, the ball deflected off my foot and into Dave's path. As Chris came in with a tackle, Dave planted the ball in the net and it was 3–0!

Mr James shouted out instructions and switched some players around. Steven came into defence with me and Jason was put into midfield. Chris was sent up to partner Abs in attack. And it worked. Within two minutes we'd scored a goal. And it was a real beauty!

It started at the back, where I won the ball from Adam and passed it to Steven. He moved out of defence and gave it to Jason, who ran past three players and played it out to Abs, who was standing on the left wing. Abs cut inside his marker and crossed the ball at knee height, to the edge of the box. Before anyone else blinked, Chris was onto the ball and he smashed a shot into their goal. 3–1! We went crazy and jumped Chris as Mr James shouted at us to calm down.

'You haven't won anything yet!' he bellowed. 'Get back to your positions and concentrate!'

We had two more chances but missed both before the whistle blew for half-time.

As we trudged off the pitch, Abs was moaning.

'That was rubbish,' he said repeatedly. '*Rubbish, rubbish, rubbish . . .*'

'We'll be OK,' I told him. 'We've started playing now and they haven't had a shot since we scored.'

'Yeah, but we've got some right potatoes playin' for us,' added Abs.

Jason smirked. 'What's with all the stupid vegetable names?' he asked Abs. 'It was cabbage-face before, and now potatoes . . . you got any funny ones?'

'Yeah,' said Abs, grinning. 'How about . . . Jason?'

'Get lost!'

I shook my head and sat down at the edge of the pitch.

Mr James came over and told me to get up. 'You'll get cold sitting down,' he said to me.

He had a plastic tub with him and there were oranges inside it, cut into slices. He offered them around and then started talking to us about the first half.

'You've got to do better,' he told us. 'I know they've got that big lad with them but he's not that good . . . we need to pass the ball to each other and run more . . .'

He went on for another minute or so, telling each player what to do, before walking off to talk to Mr Turner. As I watched, they wrote some stuff down on a clipboard. And then they pointed out some of the *other* players, nodding to each other. They hadn't pointed at me or my friends, and I started to panic. What if they were picking the people who'd made the squad? Maybe we weren't going to make it. Suddenly I felt a bit sick. I turned to Chris.

'We have to do better,' I said to him as my stomach started to feel funny.

He nodded as he sucked on a slice of orange.

'*No!*' I said urgently. 'Look! They're picking the squad and they aren't looking at us.'

Chris looked over at the coaches and his face fell.

'*Nah!*' he said, after he'd spat the orange slice out.

Just then my dad and Jason's mum came over.

'Come on, lads!' said my dad, smiling. 'You're better than this.'

'Yes . . . come on!' said Jason's mum, making a fist. 'You are going to play for the Rushton Reds! Go on!' Her face was bright pink and she looked a bit scary.

'We *have* to make the team,' I said to Jason.

He looked at his mum and went red.

'She can be *so* embarrassing sometimes,' he moaned under his breath as my belly began to feel as though it was full of ants, all crawling around inside.

The second half started a few minutes later and I was determined to turn things around. The other team had made some substitutions, and I told Jason that we had to attack them from the start.

'Just get the ball to me,' he replied, 'and I'll get Abs and Chris going . . .'

It took ten minutes to find a way through the other team's defence, but when we did Abs scored a cracker with his left foot. 3–2! He went mental, running all the way back to high-five our goalkeeper. And straight from the restart, Steven won the ball and passed it to me. I ran into the opposition's half of the pitch and skipped two challenges before coming up against Adam, who had moved into midfield. He was bearing down on me like a buffalo and I started worrying that I

might lose the ball. He was steaming
towards me . . .

But just as Adam got close, Jason popped
up next to me. I squared the ball to him. He
spun round and found Abs with a great pass.
Abs already knew he was better than the
defender in front of him. He flew down to the
touchline and crossed the ball. It was sailing

through the air and I sprinted to meet it with my head. *Bang!* The ball flew into the net and my head exploded in happiness. It was 3–3! This time even Mr James was jumping up and down and cheering. I heard my dad shout, 'Nice one, son!' and then I went back to take my position.

After that the game got scrappy, and in

the end we didn't manage to find a winner. But that didn't bother me. When the final whistle blew, I was happy that we'd got the draw after being three goals down. I felt like an FA Cup-winner and as we walked off the pitch the other lads were congratulating each other.

But it didn't last very long. Mr Turner gathered all the players together and shook his head.

'Some good play,' he told us, 'but not enough. The defending was sloppy – and half of you couldn't be bothered to run. I only want *determined* players for Rushton Reds and some of you just weren't up for it. I'm going to read out thirty names. If your name is called out then you need to be back here for six p.m. on Thursday.'

I gulped down air and my stomach turned somersaults. I had to be on that list of names. Had to be!

'And if your name isn't called out, then never mind. You haven't made the squad this time. But don't give up. There are lots of other trials to attend . . . and thank you all for trying.'

Jason put his hand up to ask a question.

'What is it, son?' asked Mr James.

'Isn't thirty players a lot for one squad?' he asked.

Mr James nodded as Mr Turner explained further.

'Thursday is trial number two,' he told us. 'That's when we'll narrow the field down to sixteen players, with another four or five as standbys . . .'

I looked around. There were some *really* good players. I wasn't sure that me and *all* of my mates would make it. Mr Turner started to read out the list of names . . .

He read one name and then another. But he hadn't read my name out or any of my friends. He read out two more names. Still none of us! I started to panic and I could feel the sweat on my forehead tingling. What if we didn't make it? What were we going to do then?

That was when I heard 'Abs, Jason and Chris.'

I expected to hear my name next, but I didn't. And it wasn't the next one either. What was going on? Was I going to fail when my best friends had all made it? Would they still want to be my friends if I wasn't a Rushton Red like they were? I was starting to feel sick again. What if I was no good . . . ?

Then I heard *my* name, just as I thought my heart was going to burst out of my chest. I wanted to jump up and down but I didn't. Instead I reminded myself that I still had to pass the second trial. I couldn't see one bad player in the list for Trial Number Two. We were only over the *first* hurdle. Thursday was going to be even *more* difficult.

'Come on then, lads,' said my dad, after the coaches had left. 'Time to get home and showered. Well done!'

I looked at Abs. 'There's some good players coming back on Thursday,' I said.

'I don't care,' replied Abs. 'We'll be better than them again.'

I turned to Chris and Jason. 'What do you two think?' I asked them.

Chris shrugged and Jason shook his head.

'It's gonna be hard,' Jason said.

'Not if some of them don't make it in time,' said Chris mysteriously.

'Huh?' I asked.

'Never mind,' said Chris. 'Just leave it to me . . .'

He winked at me and then refused to tell me what he was on about all the way home.

Chapter 5

Wednesday

The next day all we talked about was football. Very soon everyone else at school started to get fed up. The first person to say something was a girl called Lily Jones. Only she wasn't actually fed up. She was just mad!

'Can't you talk about anything else?' she asked me and Jason as we sat on a wall during morning break.

Jason shrugged and asked her what she wanted to talk about. His face went a bit red because he fancied Lily.

'Oh, anything,' she replied. 'Just not football. I mean, I like football. I even play, but can't we *please* talk about music or something?'

I groaned as Jason just smiled at her. The fool.

'But you weren't even talking to us,' I said to her.

Lily grinned. 'Yeah – but I *could* have been,' she replied as one of her friends, Parvy, joined her.

'And . . . ?' I asked.

'*And* just think of all the *cool* points you could get . . .'

Parvy started to giggle.

'I mean – it's not every day that someone like *me* talks to you, is it?' Lily continued.

But I didn't have a clue what she was on about.

'Er . . .' I began.

'And with me being so beautiful and

45

clever – just think how jealous everyone else will be . . .'

She took my hand and squeezed it hard. I tried to pull it away but she held on tight. Then she kissed me on the cheek! Jason's eyes nearly popped out of his head. From behind us I heard a really irritating voice. It was Nilesh – the school geek.

'*EHHHH!*' he whined. '*Dal just kissed Lily! Dal just kissed Lily!*'

'*Dal's got a girlfriend! Dal's got a girlfriend!*' sang his silly friend, Mark.

As I pulled away from Lily she shook her head.

'Boys are *sooo* silly!' she said to Parvy as they walked away.

'What was that all about?' asked Jason.

'I don't know,' I replied, feeling embarrassed. 'She's crazy, she is.'

Jason looked kind of worried. 'Are you and her going out?' he said.

'*No!*' I said really quickly. 'I don't like girls. I only like football!'

Jason nodded at me.

'Come on,' I said. 'It's time for our next lesson.'

'I didn't know Lily played football,' said Jason as we walked in.

'There's a girls' team at the club,' I told him. 'I saw a notice about it.'

'Be funny if she played for the boys' team,' added Chris.

I gave him a look that said *forget it*.

'That's never, *ever* happening,' I replied.

We walked into our classroom and sat down. Abs and Chris were already there. They'd been helping our teacher, Mr Kilminster, with something.

'What did the Killer want you to do?' I asked Chris. Killer was Mr Kilminster's nickname.

'Nothing much,' replied Chris. 'We just

helped him move some boxes around. What did you get up to?'

'He didn't get up to much,' said Parvy from behind us. 'He was too busy kissing Lily!'

'*Eh?*' said Chris, looking shocked.

'No way!' added Abs, who'd overheard. 'Did you kiss Lily?'

I shook my head. I could feel myself going red. Why had she kissed me? I didn't even like her!

'It wasn't like that,' I explained, just as Nilesh and Mark walked in, sniggering at each other.

'He just walked up, asked her out and then kissed her,' Parvy said, lying through her teeth. 'Just like that. Didn't even buy her a pen or something first . . .'

'I was very pleased though,' said Lily from behind me.

Now my face was even redder than before.

I didn't know what to say.

'We're really happy and plan to get married as soon as we can . . .' Lily added, grinning like a cat.

'*NO!*' I shouted as Killer walked in.

'What's the matter with you, boy?' he asked me.

'Nothing, sir,' I replied.

'Good. In that case sit down and be quiet. And that goes for the rest of you too.'

'You're weird,' whispered Chris.

'I didn't do anything!' I whispered back. 'Honest!'

'DALJIT!' shouted Mr Kilminster.

'Sorry, sir,' I mumbled as Killer glared at me.

'You'd better be,' he threatened, his face going redder than a strawberry. Redder than my face too.

I looked at Lily and she blew me a kiss.

*

At lunch time I asked Chris what he'd meant after the trial.

'Eh?' he asked, looking at me like I had a sausage growing out of my head.

'You said "not if some of them don't make it in time" – *remember?*' I reminded him.

'Oh, that,' he said. 'I was just talking. I didn't mean anything by it.'

'Oh . . . never mind,' I said, trying not to sound disappointed. I had hoped that he'd have some amazing plan but he obviously didn't. 'We need to get sorted for the second trial,' I added a bit more cheerily.

Chris scratched his head. 'How?' he asked.

'I don't know. But it's going to be really difficult. We have to play better than we did.'

'We will – have faith,' he replied.

'I wish someone *could* make half of the other lads late for the trial,' I said.

'Why don't you write a letter to Santa

Claus,' suggested Chris, teasing me.

'It's not funny,' I told him. 'We *have* to be in the starting eleven on Saturday . . .'

'I wanted a hamster when I was six and my dad told me to write to Santa and I got a hamster,' Chris told me.

'Yeah,' I said. 'I remember. You let it out onto the street and it never came back, did it?'

'My dad found it,' he said. 'A car ran it over. Mum said it went to Hamster Heaven.'

I grinned.

'Adults are so *stupid* sometimes,' added Chris. 'Like there's a heaven for hamsters . . .'

I was at home with my dad, watching *The Simpsons*, when Chris called for me. I answered the door and he walked in, acting all shady, with a backpack on across his shoulders.

'What's up?' I asked.

'Can you come out for a bit?' he asked in a whisper.

'Why are you whispering?'

'Can you?' he repeated.

'I'll have to ask . . .'

My dad looked at his watch when I asked him. 'Where are you going?'

'With Chris,' I told him. 'He's in the hallway.'

Dad got up and walked out into the hallway with me.

'It's OK, Mr Singh,' Chris said when my dad asked him where we were going. 'It's just over to the church – my mum wants us to help with fundraising and there's a quick meeting today. It'll be over by seven-thirty . . .'

'Oh,' said my dad, smiling. 'That's a great idea. Something worthwhile for you layabouts to do. It'll stop you playing on those silly computers, won't it? Just make sure you both get home on time, OK?'

'Thanks, Dad!' I beamed.

'And call me if you need a lift,' he said.

'OK,' I replied as I followed Chris out of the front door.

I waited until we were three houses away before I pulled my best friend up.

'What are you on about?' I asked. 'What fundraising?'

Chris grinned. 'Relax,' he told me. 'We're going to help a good cause. *Our* cause.'

He didn't say anything else until we got to the end of the road. Abs and Jason were waiting there for us. They looked as puzzled as me.

'This better be good,' Abs warned Chris.

'My mum didn't want me to come so I had to get my dad to say yes.'

'Yeah,' added Jason. 'My mum isn't happy either. I have to be home for seven-thirty dead on . . .'

Chris pulled the backpack off his shoulders.

It was black with two red straps. He unzipped it and pulled out a roll of posters. As the rest of us looked at each other, he unrolled the posters and showed one to us. It was handwritten, in huge letters, and then scanned and photocopied . . .

IMPORTANT!/////////////////
FOOTBALL TRIAL CHANGED TO 7 P.M.

I shook my head. 'Are you bonkers?' I asked Chris.

'It'll work,' he said. 'All we have to do is put these up all over the place and half the lads won't turn up until it's too late.'

Abs started laughing.

'What if they don't see the poster?' asked Jason.

'If only five of them see it, that's five *less* people to compete against,' Chris said.

You're *stupid*!' Abs told him.

'Well, I don't see *you* doing anything to help,' Chris said back. He looked a bit hurt.

I looked at the poster again and felt the familiar knot in my stomach. I had to make the final team, but this wasn't the way we were supposed to do it.

'We *could* try it,' I heard myself say. 'I mean, the trial is tomorrow so it might not even work, but what's the harm in trying?'

Jason looked unsure. 'It's a bit like cheating though, isn't it?' he asked.

'How?' asked Chris.

'Well, we should be in the starting eleven because we're the best ones. Not because we've tricked people,' he explained.

'Oh, let's just put them up,' said Abs suddenly.

'Changed your tune now?' asked Chris. 'Shouldn't expect anything less from a Man Poo fan . . .'

'They aren't going to work,' Abs said.

'Just like Liverpool's strikers. But that don't stop the manager from putting *them* out.' He started laughing at his own joke.

'Come on then,' I said. 'Let's do it!'

Chapter 6

Thursday

We put the posters up everywhere. On lamp-posts, bins, bus stops. We even stuck one on the notice board outside the local church. Then we all ran home. I tried not to think about it all the next day – the posters or the trial.

Six o'clock came round so quickly but our scam hadn't made any difference. By the time we got to the youth club all the lads from the first trial were already there. And Mr Turner was standing with a group of parents staring at one of our posters.

'I really don't know,' I heard him say as I walked over to where he was standing.

'They were everywhere, Steve,' added one of the parents, a tall man with grey hair.

'It's very strange,' continued Mr Turner. 'I didn't change the time and nor did Ian James, so I can't for the life of me understand why—'

That was all I heard because I walked away to go and tell the others what had happened.

'It didn't work,' I said to them.

'Knew it wouldn't,' replied Abs. 'It was a stupid idea. Just like making a football team called Liverpool—'

'Shut up, you chav!' Chris shouted.

I sighed. 'Can we just concentrate on the trial?' I asked.

Jason nodded. 'Yeah. It doesn't matter

about the posters. It was cheating anyway,'
he said.

'But I did it for all of us,' said Chris. 'And
how was I supposed to know it wasn't going
to work?'

'Who cares?' replied Abs, in his usual
cocky way. 'We're gonna get into the starting
eleven – trust me . . .'

'Bit hard to trust a Man Poo fan,' I said.

'Least I ain't got a face like a toilet brush,'
replied Abs.

As we walked into the changing rooms at
the clubhouse, Jason asked Abs how
someone could have a face like a toilet
brush.

'Just look in the mirror,' he replied,
giggling at his own joke. As usual.

The other lads were already changing when
we got inside and I ended up getting ready
between Steven and Adam – the big lad.

'You're back!?' Adam said, smirking. 'I

thought only the good players could come back?'

I gave him a funny look. 'What does that mean, mate?!'

Adam just went on, 'I didn't play my best last time so I'm going to be even better this time,' he said.

'That wouldn't be hard,' Chris said from the bench opposite.

'We'll see,' Adam warned.

In my head I was worried about what Adam had said. He was so much bigger than the rest of us. And if he had a problem with me, what could I do about it? I didn't want him to know I was worried though. So I tried to see if I could wind him up. He'd started on me so it was fair game.

'There's girls I know that play better than you,' I said.

Adam spun round and faced up to me.

'You what?' he said, screwing up his face.

'*Girls*,' Chris told him. 'You know, them people that don't have anything to do with ugly freaks like you?'

I could see that Adam was getting angrier and I wondered whether we should stop pushing him but Chris didn't care.

'And how big *are* your feet anyway?' he asked Adam. 'Munster or Shrek size?'

Adam clenched his fists by his side. They were huge. 'You're gonna regret saying that!' he told Chris. 'Even if I don't get into *this* team. It ain't the *only* team in the league . . .'

'Yeah, but it's gonna be the *best*,' I told him. 'With me and my mates playing . . .'

'You lot couldn't hit a cow's bum with a banjo,' he said, smirking again.

'We're gonna make you lot look like girls!' Jason said from behind us.

Adam started to go for Jason just as the two coaches walked in.

'Something wrong?' Mr Turner asked sternly.

'No – nothing,' said Adam.

'Just messing about,' Chris told the coach.

'Well, stop it and get outside. This trial should have started ten minutes ago.'

'What were those posters about?' I asked Mr James.

'Just a misunderstanding,' he replied. 'Probably some kids messing about. Our rivals, Evington Eagles, up to no good, I suspect . . .'

I nodded, pleased that we'd got away with our rubbish plan. And I also started wondering about the Evington Eagles. Neither coach had mentioned them before. Why were they our deadliest rivals? Was it like Liverpool versus Everton – a local derby? Evington was the area next to ours so I guessed it was. Suddenly I got really excited and couldn't wait to get out onto the pitch.

'Only fifteen minutes' warm-up today and then straight into eleven versus eleven,' Mr James told us. 'And we've kept the teams similar to the other day. Adam will captain one and Jason the other. As before – if you don't start the game, keep warm and be ready to come on at any time.'

We all nodded.

'And today *is* selection day,' added Mr Turner. 'Today is when we pick the squad for the Rushton Reds.'

I gulped. Was I going to be good enough to make it?

The pitch was heavy as it had been raining during the afternoon. I could smell the grass and the mud. I jogged over to the centre circle, quickly joined by the others.

'Single file!' shouted Mr James. 'A slow jog along the marked lines. Stay behind the man in front of you.'

He set off with the rest of us behind him, running the lines in a random pattern. After five minutes we lined up along the touchline and raced each other in sprints to the halfway line. All the while I was watching Adam to see how he was doing. And from what I could tell, he was keeping an eye on me and Chris, who was running beside me. Once when I looked across at him, he smirked and made a fist. I nodded at him, not wanting to let him see that I was bothered.

After the warm-up, we split into two teams with substitutes. Me, Chris, Jason and Abs were on the same side again, along with Gurinder and Steven. There were some other lads as well and two of them had been on the opposite side last time around. One of them came up and offered me his hand to shake. He was short and skinny with spiky brown hair that had been gelled stiff.

'I'm Corky,' he told me. 'You were really good last time.'

'Thanks,' I said, smiling. 'I'm Dal – and these lads are . . .'

I introduced him to the rest of the lads.

'This is Leon,' said Corky, introducing us to the player next to him. 'He couldn't make it the other night but Mr Turner let him come today anyway.'

Leon was taller and he had his hair in small braids, tight against his head.

'Easy,' Leon said to all of us.

'Easy yourself with your girlie haircut,' Chris shouted back.

I turned and gave my best mate a dirty look. What did he think he was doing? But Chris just grinned at me, and when I turned to look at Leon, instead of getting upset or angry, he was grinning too.

'Chris is my cousin,' Leon told us. 'Although he comes from the ugly side of the family . . .'

I laughed.

'Let's get some tactics sorted, lads,' said Mr James as he came towards us. Behind him was a woman: a very pretty woman with long brown hair and a big smile.

'This is Miss Rice,' Mr James told us. 'She coaches the girls' team and helps out with ours too.'

'Hey, boys,' said Miss Rice. 'We ready to play soccer?'

Her accent was American. Steven nudged me in the back and then spoke up.

'It's football, miss.'

'Football, soccer . . .' replied Miss Rice. 'Really – who cares? The question is, can you all play the game?'

Some of the other lads shouted out 'Woo!' as Steven went a bit red.

'Right, let's be having you . . .' said Mr James.

He quickly read out the starting positions

and names. I was in defence and I smiled
when I saw that Steven was put in next to
me. Corky got the position just in front of
us, alongside Jason. Abs and Chris were
up front with Leon on the right and Gurinder
in goal. The rest of the lads filled in the
other positions and we had four substitutes.
As we took up positions Corky pulled me
aside.

'Watch out for that big lad, Adam,' he
told me.

I nodded. 'He's good, isn't he?' I said.

Corky shook his head. That wasn't what he meant. 'He trained for the Eagles yesterday too,' he said. 'My brother saw him. And he was going on about getting you and your mates – in the changing room earlier.'

I nodded again. 'Can he train for us *and* the Eagles?' I asked.

'Only if no one finds out about it,' replied Corky, winking at me. 'I did trials for Clarendon United too.'

'Who are they?' I asked. All I knew was that Clarendon was one of the areas next to ours. I didn't know anything about their team.

'They're the best team in the league along with the Eagles,' replied Corky.

'So how come you're training with us?' I asked him, getting suspicious.

He grinned at me. 'They told me I wasn't good enough to play for them,' he admitted. 'And now I'm going to join the Reds and prove them wrong! That's who we're playing on Saturday and I'm going to score against them!'

I looked at him and wished I could be as determined as he was. But I was really, really nervous . . .

Chapter 7

The first ten minutes went OK. Neither team scored but ours had the best chances. We were passing the ball around well and I could tell that Mr James was happy with us. He was standing on the side with Miss Rice and he kept on pointing players out and nodding his head. The other team were just kicking the ball anywhere, but we were making sure that we passed accurately. Then we had a break on the left and Jason picked up the ball.

One of their defenders closed him down but Jason just waited for him to get close and then slid the ball between his legs, the classic nutmeg move. He looked up and saw me in the middle of the pitch. He played the ball to me at speed. I took it with my right foot but didn't control it properly. It shot out to my right and I had to stretch to get control of it. But when I did I saw Abs out of the corner of my eye. He was running into space, with nothing between him and the goal. I knew one of their players was closing in on me, but I waited a few moments before sliding the ball through to Abs.

I didn't have time to admire my pass though. As soon as I played the ball, someone steamed into me from the side and my legs came out from underneath me. I hit the ground and got a mouthful of mud. I rolled over twice as a shooting pain worked its way up my left shin.

'*OWW!!!!!!!!!!!*' I cried out.

I heard the whistle go and then one of my team-mates shouting. It was Chris and he was having a go at someone.

'That's a bad tackle!' he complained. 'He didn't even go for the ball!'

'I'll deal with it,' I heard Mr Turner say.

I rolled over again and saw the ref call Adam over. Slowly, I got to my feet. My shin was aching but it wasn't too bad. I walked around a bit, trying to shake it off. Mr Turner was talking to Adam.

'There was no need for that, son,' he told him. 'The ball had gone—'

'Yeah, but—' began Adam.

'Just listen!' warned Mr Turner. 'I'm not having any more of that. Stay on your feet and don't go diving in . . . OK?'

'OK,' moaned Adam. He turned and walked back to his position, right past me. 'Next time I'll get you properly,' he snarled.

I shrugged at him and half walked, half limped back to my position. The free kick I'd been given was taken by Steven, who passed the ball left to Leon. Leon controlled it and pushed it into the space in front of him. He set off after it with a defender trying to catch him. But Leon was too quick and he reached the ball first. He looked up and then squared the ball to Abs. I heard Chris, who was behind Abs, shout, 'Leave it!' Abs let it go through his legs, which fooled their defence, and Chris was suddenly in on goal. With Adam trying desperately to hold him back, he side-footed the ball past their keeper.

1–0!

Chris turned to Adam. 'That's for my mate!' he jeered. 'Cheers!'

Then he was mobbed by our team.

The game went on for another ten minutes before we got our next chance. But this time

Chris didn't get hold of the ball properly and Adam managed to clear it away. Then the opposition got a lucky break. Jason was trying to pass the ball to Corky when it hit the ref and rebounded to Adam instead. He set off at a sprint, the ball at his huge feet. First Steven and then Corky tried to stop him but he just shrugged them both off. Our right back, a lad called Tony, got in his way, but Adam dribbled past him too.

I was next. I moved towards Adam, keeping my eyes fixed firmly on the ball. He turned it left but I was there so he moved it to the right. But I was too quick again and he had to hold back. He stopped, waited for me to come in with a challenge and then set off again, leaving me flat-footed for a second. But I woke up quickly and tried to catch him again. I kept my eyes on the ball, and just as he was about to shoot for goal I slid out my right foot and took the ball away cleanly.

'*ARRGHHHH!*' screamed Adam, diving to the floor.

I rolled around and got straight to my feet. Adam did the same. And then he was in my face, calling me a cheat. Mr Turner blew his whistle and then ran over to us.

'Clean tackle, clean tackle!' he said.

'You fouled me!' Adam said, pointing at me.

'I won the ball,' I replied, staying calm.

I could see that Adam was really angry, and I knew that if he kicked off he'd be sent off the pitch. I remembered what Corky had told me and the foul he'd committed on me earlier. I decided to try and wind him up. I smirked at him and then made a diving gesture with my hands.

'You what?' he shouted, grabbing out at my shirt. I felt a bolt of fear streak through me and looked up at him. It was like staring up a cliff face at a gorilla.

'LEAVE IT!' shouted Mr Turner. 'Get back

to your position, son!'

Adam kind of growled at me but he did as he was told.

'Drop ball to restart,' Mr Turner said when things had calmed down.

The first half ended 1–0 to us. But as soon as the second half started, their strikers, Dave and Harry, combined and scored a great goal. We hadn't even had time to think and they were celebrating the equalizer.

'Concentrate!' Mr James shouted from the sidelines.

'Get tighter to their attack!' Miss Rice shouted at me and Steven.

I turned to her and held up my thumb to say OK. She held a thumb up too and smiled at me.

'You're doing really well,' she said as I went to get the ball at a throw-in a few moments later. 'Keep going . . .'

But that wasn't easy to do. Adam had moved into midfield, and for some reason each time I looked up he was close by. I grabbed Steven.

'That Adam's got it in for me,' I told him. 'Cover me.'

'No worries, mate,' replied Steven. 'I got him.'

We gave away a free kick just outside our eighteen-yard area and as I looked for someone to mark, I saw Adam. He was standing on the six-yard line with his hand up in the air. I walked over and stood between him and the goal. He nudged me with his shoulder. It felt like it was made of rock. But I didn't chicken out. I nudged him back.

'I'm gonna score from this,' he hissed to me. 'You ain't stopping me . . .'

I nodded but kept quiet. Suddenly I felt a presence at my side. It was Steven.

And behind him, standing by the goalpost,

was Abs. I got ready for the ball to come into the box, but it didn't. As Adam pushed me out of the way, the ball sailed harmlessly wide. That didn't stop Adam though. He pushed me forward and into the ground and landed on top of me. As he did so, he dug his elbow into my ribs and my face into the grass.

'*AGHHH!!!!*' I groaned as I tasted mud for the second time. And then the wind just disappeared out of my lungs.

All around me it went off. Adam was having a go at Steven, who had pushed him. And Adam's team-mates, Harry and Dave, joined in, with Chris and Abs having a go too. I heard the whistle go a few times and then I heard Adam call Mr Turner names.

'RIGHT!' I heard Mr Turner say as I slowly got my breath back. 'I don't want a thug like you in my team. You're *off*!'

As I sat up to take some more air in,

Adam leaned over and spoke to me.

'Didn't wanna play for this team anyway,' he said. 'I'm goin' to the Eagles.'

'Lucky you,' I said, trying not to grimace as my ribs throbbed.

'Look out for me,' he warned. 'I'm not done with you yet . . .'

And then he walked off, calling our team a bunch of girls. His two mates, Dave and Harry, went after him and finally, after I'd had time to recover a bit, Mr Turner told us he'd seen enough.

'Trial's over,' he said. 'Go and get changed. Mr James and I will be in shortly.'

We didn't have to wait long. Mr Turner did the same as he had after the first trial. We stood and waited nervously as he read out each name slowly. Once again I didn't hear my name. He'd called out eight names before one of my friends was called out. That was Jason, who shouted 'YES!' when he heard his name.

Then Mr Turner called out the names Leon, Corky, Steven and Gurinder, one after the other. There were only three names left to call out and me, Chris and Abs were still waiting. I had a bad feeling in my belly. I hadn't made it . . .

'Chris,' said Mr Turner.

Chris looked at me and shrugged, as if to say 'Sorry, mate'. I wanted to be sick. I had to be in the squad.

'Abs,' Mr Turner added a moment later.

Abs jumped up and down on the spot, whooping with delight. But then he saw my face and he stopped. There was one name left to call out and too many boys waiting to be told! I hadn't made it. All my friends were in the team and I was going to have to forget about it . . .

'And . . . Dal,' Mr Turner called out after

what seemed like five years!

'YES!' I shouted. *'Yes, yes, yes!!!!!!!!!!!!!!!!'*

After congratulating us and saying well done to the boys who hadn't made it, Mr Turner told us to be back at 9 a.m. on Saturday.

'We're going to do warm-ups and tactics before the game against Clarendon United, which kicks off at eleven.'

I sat down on a bench, holding my sore ribs.

'You gonna be OK?' Steven asked me.

'Yeah – just a bruise or two,' I told him.

'Forget the bruises,' said Chris. 'We did it!'

'We're all Rushton REDS!' Jason sang out. 'RUSHIE REDS, RUSHIE REDS, RUSHIE REDS!!!!!!!!!!!!!!!!!!'

I sat down on a bench and smiled, relieved that I had made it. It felt great!

Chapter 8

Saturday

It was cold and wet when we turned up for our first game. Abs was actually shivering and Jason had a bit of a cold. His nose was red and snotty. He was sniffing constantly.

'It's *freezing*,' said Chris as we walked towards the changing rooms.

'Like Eskimo cold,' I replied.

'Bet the inside of the clubhouse is going to *feel* like an igloo too,' added Abs.

When we got inside we found three of the squad waiting for us. One of them nodded to us.

'All right?' he said. He was called Byron and the lads with him were Pete and Ben.

I said hello as Steven and Gurinder walked in too. We sat down and started talking about the game.

'Who we playing today?' asked Jason. 'What are they like?'

'Clarendon United,' Byron told him. 'They're really good.'

'How d'you know that?' asked Abs.

'My brother used to play for them,' explained Byron. 'They've got loads of teams; right up to adults.'

I watched as some more lads walked in.

One of them – a tall lad with blond hair and freckles – I knew already. His name was Anthony, although everyone called him Ant. He was followed in by Rajvir and Will, two lads I hadn't met before the trials.

'Corky told me that Clarendon are the best team in the league along with

Evington Eagles,' I told everyone.

Ant nodded and then rubbed his hands together. 'Clarendon won the league last year and the Eagles won the City Cup,' he replied. 'And they're our two closest rivals.'

'If we can beat *them*,' added Ben, 'then we can beat *any* of the other teams.'

Chris and me nodded at the same time.

By the time Leon and Corky arrived, Mr Turner was already going through some tactics. They were closely followed by two lads who looked the same. Twins called Alfie and Tom. When the whole squad had taken a seat, Mr Turner continued.

'OK, lads, let's get down to it . . .'

Alfie held up his hand.

'Yes, Alfie?' asked Mr Turner.

'Tom and I are injured,' replied Alfie.

'Oh – OK. What's the problem?'

'We were playing football at home and

hurt our shins – they're really badly bruised,' explained Tom.

'*Both* of you?' asked Mr Turner.

They nodded together.

'At the *same* time?' asked Chris, grinning.

They nodded again.

'Oh,' said Mr Turner. 'Anyone else got an injury?'

I turned and looked at the rest of the squad. I wasn't expecting anyone else to put their hands up. But I was about to get a shock. Rajvir, Will, Pete and Ben all put their hands up. That meant we were down to *ten* players and *no* substitutes. It was unbelievable!

'Right,' said Mr Turner. 'Looks like we've got a problem before we've even begun . . .'

Jason put up his hand.

'You're not going to tell me that *you're* injured too, are you?' said Mr Turner.

'No, sir. I just wanted to know how

we're going to play with ten men?'

Mr Turner smiled. '*Well . . .*' he began as Mr James and Miss Rice walked in too, 'there is something I wanted to tell you all at the trial . . .'

'We've got two extra players with two more on their way,' added Miss Rice.

'Nice one!' said Chris. 'Where are they?'

'Getting changed,' said Mr James, 'which is what you lot should be doing.'

Abs looked from me to Chris to Jason.

'Why are they getting changed somewhere else?'

This time Miss Rice cracked a big smile. She looked at Mr Turner, who nodded.

'Because they're members of *my* team,' she told us.

'*Your team?*' I blurted out. 'But *your* team are—'

'Yes, I know,' she said, cutting me off. 'My team are *girls*!'

'*NO WAY!*' shouted Abs. 'No way, no way, no way!'

We were still moaning about girls playing with us when we got outside. Well, Abs and Steven were. But that wasn't going to be the last surprise. The girls hadn't come out yet, so we were doing stretches by the side of the pitch, led by Mr James.

'We're gonna get thumped,' said Abs.

'And laughed at,' said Steven. 'The shame . . .'

'They should have told us,' added Chris. 'I mean, that's not fair, is it – just telling us like that?'

Mr James told us to stop and gather round. There were a lot of disgruntled faces.

'Listen, lads,' he began. 'I know it's not what you were expecting, but we think that it'll be really good for the team.'

'Why?' asked Corky. 'Because we'll get beat every week?'

Mr James shook his head. 'One of the reasons you made the squad, Corky, was because you looked like a battler during the trial – now you're just being negative . . .'

'But he's right,' I told Mr James. 'Boys and girls don't play together. They're just not as good as us.'

'You might live to regret those words, Dal,' replied Mr James. 'The girls we've chosen are fantastic players.'

'No way!' said Byron. 'One tackle and they'll run home crying . . .'

'And what happens if they break a nail?' asked Chris. 'My sister cried for two days when she broke one of hers.'

'Yeah, but your sister's mental,' said Abs.

'Good point,' replied Chris, grinning.

'Just give them a chance,' pleaded

Mr James. 'You haven't even met them or seen them play yet.'

'Sir, where's your accent from?' asked Jason, totally randomly.

'Middlesbrough, son . . .'

'Are they like Newcastle?' asked Abs cheekily. He knew that Newcastle and Middlesbrough were big rivals.

'Leave it, Abs, or you'll spend the rest of the morning doing press-ups,' said Mr James. Only he was smiling when he said it. Lucky Abs.

We went through forty more minutes of training and working with the practice footballs. It involved lots of short sprints and stretching exercises and then a long run around the edges of the pitch. As our muscles warmed up, I wondered where the girls were.

'I thought the girls were here?' I asked Mr James.

'They are, son,' he replied. 'Miss Rice has them warming up inside.'

'See?' said Abs, looking upset. 'They're already getting treated better than us!'

'They're just going through the same thing as you are,' said Mr James. 'And Miss Rice knows what she's doing. Her team were league champions last season.'

'Yeah, but that was in the Barbie league,' joked Chris.

'Let's just give them a chance, lads,' replied Mr James.

At the end of training Mr James told us to keep warm and practise with the balls in any way we wanted to. Freestyle, he called it. I teamed up with Chris and Byron and we formed a triangle and began to pass the ball to each other, with only two touches allowed. On my fifth pass I looked up to play the ball to Chris. But he was just grinning like a crazy man. And then he burst into laughter.

'What's up with you?' I asked as someone came up behind me and tapped my shoulder.

'*Oi!*' I said, spinning round and coming face to face with Lily and Parvy. They were both wearing football kit and boots.

'Hello, my darling boyfriend,' said Lily with a huge grin. 'Shall we *play* . . . ?'

Chapter 9

By the time I'd got over my shock we were on the pitch, ready to kick off against Clarendon United. My dad was watching from the sidelines and he waved at me and shouted encouragement. Chris's and Abs's dads were there too, alongside Jason's mum.

'You can do it, son!' my dad shouted at me.

I nodded and held my thumb up to him. Then I turned and looked around at my team-mates. Lily was playing in midfield with Jason, Byron and Corky. I was at the back alongside Steven, with Leon on the right and Parvy on the left. Up front were Abs and Chris, and Gurinder was in goal. The subs were Ant and the twins, even though they were injured, and two more girls, Emma and Penny.

'We're in trouble,' said Byron as I stood behind him.

'Positive,' I replied. 'We've got to be positive . . .'

Only it was hard to be positive. When Clarendon United's players had seen that we had girls in our team, they started laughing at us. Some of them were taunting us, asking if we all had to wear skirts and stuff like that. Mr Turner had used it in the final team talk, telling us to remember their annoying taunts so we'd try even harder.

'You're a *team*,' he told us. 'You *play* for each other and you *back* each other up – no matter what.'

Now as we stood in the rain, waiting for the whistle to start the game, I wasn't at all confident. In fact, I was expecting to lose. But I tried to shake off the negative feeling. My dad had always taught me to be positive, in any situation. If you believed you were going to lose before you started, you'd already lost.

'Come on, lads!' I shouted out, trying to get them going.

'Er . . . ?' said Lily, turning to me.

'And girls!' I added.

'What a bunch of losers!' shouted one of United's players, a tall lad with long brown hair and zits on his forehead.

'COME ON, YOU REDS!!!!!!!!!!' I heard my dad sing out. Then Chris's dad joined in too. We really were in a proper game! I took a deep breath and focused as Mr Turner, who was referee, blew on his whistle.

*

We did OK for the first fifteen minutes. Because we hadn't played together before, there was a lot of simple passing, just like Mr James and Miss Rice had told us to do. We even had a couple of shots on goal but Chris missed with both of them. After about twenty minutes though, Clarendon started to get better. They were trying to get the ball out to their right wing, where they had a fast and skilful winger. He was playing against Parvy. I nudged Steven and nodded towards Parvy.

'They're trying to get to her,' I said. Steven nodded. The ball had gone out for a throw-in to us and I trotted over to take it. Miss Rice was waiting for me.

'Get some support in there for Parvy,' she told me. 'Don't let her get isolated, OK, Dal?'

'No problem, miss,' I replied, throwing the ball to Jason.

Jason swivelled and ran down the left before passing the ball inside to Abs. Abs waited for a second, knowing that there was a defender coming. Then he went to go left but switched at the last minute and the defender got caught out. He skidded through the mud and landed on his backside. Abs grinned and went on a run, taking two more of their players with him. Then he was at the by-line.

He saw Byron making a run into the box and crossed so that Byron could just push the ball into the net. But Byron missed it and the ball fell to Lily. As she brought it under control, one of their defenders ran at her, making a growling noise. He was trying to scare her, put her off. But as we all watched, Lily waited until he got close, flicked the ball over his head and ran around him. She didn't wait for the ball to hit the ground. Instead she volleyed it back towards Byron.

This time he controlled it and passed it to his left. Quick as a flash Chris appeared and tapped the ball home underneath their goalie.

'YESSSS!!!!!!!!!!!!' I shouted, pumping my fist in the air.

1–0!

We ended the half a goal up. But early in the second half they equalized from a corner. I tried desperately to reach the ball, but it went over my head and fell at the feet of one of their best players. As Steven tried to block him, he smashed the ball home and then turned to me.

'*Have that!*' he shouted. 'Come on, lads – we're not getting beat by a bunch of girls!'

We tried to get it back together but suddenly we couldn't pass the ball properly and our teamwork just failed. I got the ball in defence and ran out with it, sidestepping a

few challenges. Then I played the ball square to Corky, who was desperate to score. He played a one-two with Jason and when he got the ball back Abs started calling for it. But Corky ignored him and Lily too. He looked up and saw the goal in front of him. He was still quite far out but he swung back his left foot and took a shot. His right foot slipped in the mud though, just as he made contact with the ball. The ball went horribly wide and the Clarendon players all ran to Corky and made fun of him.

'We knew you were rubbish!' said one lad.

'Had to join a girls' team,' said another lad. 'Now he's shooting like a girl too.'

I could see Corky was getting angry and so could Leon and Byron. All three of us ran over to him and calmed him down. But things just got worse after that. Soon Clarendon United had scored another two goals. By the full-time whistle, we were cold, wet, muddy and down.

'That'll teach you to play with girls,' said one of their players as we trudged off.

'Three–one!'

'Yeah,' said another United player. 'Go put your skirts back on!'

I spun round to say something but Miss Rice caught hold of me.

'Let them gloat,' she told me. 'A few more games and we'll be right up there – you'll see . . .'

I shook my head. 'We should have done better,' I said.

'Yes, and next time you will,' she told me. 'It's early days. The soccer season is long and hard. Never mind about today. We'll get it right next time. Now, go get showered.'

Once everyone was dressed, Mr Turner called us all into the main part of the building which was a community centre. He sat us down and told us that we'd done very well.

'But we got thumped!' complained Corky.

'Yes – but you played for each other. As the games continue, we'll get better,' promised Mr Turner. 'The more we practise together, the better we'll be.'

'Oh, and one more thing,' added Mr James. 'There'll be a television crew at Tuesday's training. I've got consent forms for you to give to your parents. If you want to be part of the TV thing, you need to get these signed and bring them back to me on Tuesday.'

I looked over at Chris, who shrugged.

'What's the TV thing about?' I asked.

'Just wait and see,' said Miss Rice. 'All will be explained next week . . .'

*

Lily and Parvy stood in the car park with us as we waited for lifts home. The rain had stopped and the sun was trying to peek through the clouds. But it was still windy and cold.

'So, did we play well then?' asked Parvy.

'No!' said Abs, being childish.

'Don't be like that!' said Jason. 'You did OK.'

'Yeah,' added Abs. 'But if we'd had all boys we wouldn't have lost . . .'

'We all played OK,' said Chris. 'But not good. Abs is just being silly.'

'Yeah – we'll just have to do better next week,' I added.

'*You* will,' said Lily. 'You need to stop running like a headless chicken and pass me the ball more . . .'

'Why?' I asked.

'Because, my dear, I'm better than you,' she explained.

'Don't call me that!' I moaned.

She pinched my left cheek. 'Don't be like that,' she said in a baby voice.

'*OWW!* Gerroff – that hurts!' I shouted.

'Oh, don't be such a wimp,' said Parvy.

'Yeah, Dal,' added Chris. 'You'll want to wear a skirt next . . .'

As they all burst into laughter, I rubbed my cheek and wondered what would happen in the next game. Would we win or lose? And what was the TV thing about? I turned to my friends.

'Are you all OK for training on Tuesday?' I asked.

'*YEAH!!!!*' said everyone apart from Jason.

'*Rushie Reds, Rushie Reds, Rushie Reds!*' he sang.

'Oh, do stop singing,' Lily told him.

I looked at Lily and she blew me a kiss.

'Are *you* coming too?' I asked, hoping that she'd say no.

'Of *course*, darling,' she replied. Why did she have to speak to me like *that*? I felt my face turn the colour of beetroot. Lily walked off and joined her mum, who was talking to Miss Rice.

'Great,' I said to her just before she went, but I didn't mean it. I was just praying for my dad to stop talking to the other parents and take me home.

Not that I was *too* desperate to get away. It *had* been great fun. I'd made the squad and been picked for the starting eleven. We might have lost our first game but we were definitely going to get better.

Rushton Reds were going to be the best soccer squad in the whole league. And me and my friends were going to be right at the heart of the team. I'd spent ages wanting to be part of a team, playing proper games.

And now I had that chance I wasn't going to lose it.

I was a Rushton Red!

'You OK, Dal?' asked my dad. I hadn't even noticed him walk over to me. I'd been too busy daydreaming.

'Yeah!' I said, beaming. 'I'm great!'

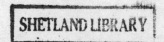
SHETLAND LIBRARY